Cat, Mouse and Moon

Roxanne Dyer Powell

Illustrated by Will Hillenbrand

Houghton Mifflin Company

Boston 1994

To Jimmy with love, for his tireless encouragement, friendship and advice;
and to Mouse, my very own Day Cat / Night Cat

—R.P.

To Amelia (Mimi) Burris and her cat, Smoky Grey

—W.H.

Text copyright © 1994 by Roxanne Dyer Powell
Illustrations copyright © 1994 by Will Hillenbrand

Library of Congress Cataloging-in-Publication Data

Powell, Roxanne Dyer.
  Cat, Mouse and Moon / Roxanne Dyer Powell ; illustrated by Will
Hillenbrand.
    p.   cm.
    Summary: Night Cat is a different creature from harmless Day Cat,
as he prowls beneath the moon stealthily stalking Mouse.
    ISBN 0-395-59348-4
    1. Cats—Juvenile fiction. [1. Cats—Fiction.]   I. Hillenbrand,
Will, ill.   II. Title.
PZ10.3.P513Cat   1994   91-42171
[E]—dc20   CIP
                             AC

Printed in the United States of America

HOR   10   9   8   7   6   5   4   3   2   1

Cat, Mouse and Moon

It is night and Cat is out. Moon is in the sky, and in Cat's eye, and on the rippling surface of the lake.

Clouds fold themselves over Moon. Sometimes they are sheer veils; other times, they are thick cloaks. When Moon breaks free of them, the night is almost as bright as day.

Cat follows Moon's path down to the water's edge.
Above Cat, Owl rests against Moon in the fork of the oak tree
where he is blinking himself awake.

Cat skirts along the edge of the pond. Moon looks over Cat's shoulder. Cat listens for anything small to make a sound. His eyes search out any movement in the darkness. Nearly everything interests a Night Cat.

"I am a mighty hunter," Cat brags to himself as he flows like black ink along the lake path.

Cat does not care if anyone agrees with him. Cat always agrees with himself.

Cat moves stealthily, softly. His tail twitches when he is paying attention. It jerks when he is not thinking of anything. Even if Cat thought about his tail, he could not stop moving it. But Cat is not thinking about his tail tonight. Cat stops.

His ears move like antennae, first one way, then the other. There, in the grass among the leaves, something is making a sound that only Cat can hear. Cat's tail twitches faster. His whiskers twitch. No other part of Cat moves.

Moon burns in Cat's eyes like live fire. Now Cat sees what is making the sound. Cat's eyes become glowing saucers and a small whitefoot mouse is trapped in the middle of them.

The mouse is cleaning his burrow near the old root of a sleepy pine tree. Mouse is too busy fussing and digging and moving pine needles about to know Cat is near, watching his every move. Mouse's back is turned toward Cat. Cat waits and licks his lips, thinking of the nice dinner he will have.

Now thick clouds wrap Moon up and steal his light. Deep night shadows reach from their hiding places behind the trees.

Nothing can see Cat, black in the black night. Cat is ready.

Cat crouches low like a coiled spring. Cat and Mouse are alone in the night.

Cat is watching Mouse. Cat thinks no one is watching him. But Cat is wrong.

Moon is watching.

Moon throws off his cloud-cloaks and floods the night with light. Under the dark limbs of the pine tree where Mouse is working, Moon becomes tiny specks in the edges of Mouse's black-bead eyes. Mouse sees Moon ruffling the edges of Cat's fur.

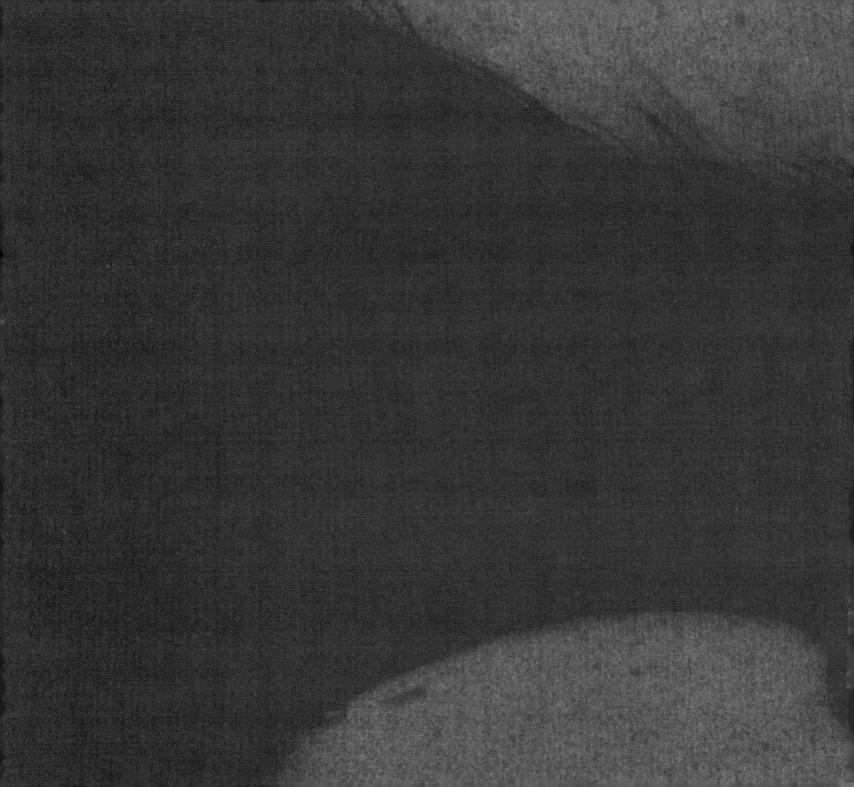

Quicker than quick, Cat springs forward with raking claws.
Quicker by a mouse's hair than Cat, Mouse dives deep into his burrow.

Mouse feels Cat strike the empty air behind him. Mouse's hairs stand on end for a moment while he breathes hard inside his safe burrow. A narrow escape, but Cat has missed him.

Cat snarls up at Moon.

Moon only beams down on Cat and the world and says nothing.

Cat's whiskers jerk from side to side with the thought of the fine dinner he almost tasted. His tail jerks with aggravation.

Cat sits near Mouse's burrow and licks his paws awhile to calm himself. He pretends not to be interested in Mouse anymore.

He secretly hopes Mouse will be careless and come outside again. It is not easy for a Night Cat to stay in one place, but Cat waits a long time.

Finally, Cat decides Mouse has seen enough of Moon tonight, and gives up.

Moon has dropped low in the sky and Cat is far from home.

Cat stretches up like a band of elastic and pads on silent rubber feet along the lake path.

Cat is hungry now and in a hurry. He hardly notices when fat Cricket plumps down in his path before hopping into the tall grasses.

He pays no attention to Owl, settling down to his daytime sleep in the oak tree.

Sun is hunched at the edge of the world like a golden lion when Cat walks up to the back step of his home. Pale Moon is tucking himself into bed as far away from Sun as he can get.

Cat catches the screen in his claws and lets the door slam with a bang. Someone opens the door and pours Cat a saucer of milk. Hands rub Cat's head and tame his ears. He closes his eyes and purrs. He is a Day Cat now.

Cat licks his milk daintily, then washes his face and paws carefully with his rough tongue. He climbs into his flannel-lined basket for a nap.

Cat sleeps peacefully. His whiskers are still and his tail hardly moves. He is as harmless as any Day Cat. But he is dreaming Night Cat dreams.

He dreams of hunting at night.
He dreams of Moon—in the sky, and in his eye, and on the
rippling surface of the lake.